The Bus Stop

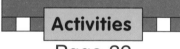

One morning, Duck sat on the bench and looked for the bus.

Duck sat and sat, but he did not see the bus.

So Duck got up to play!

Duck played on a big hill and fell into the sand.

Duck played in the green grass
and fell into the mud.

Duck played in the plants and fell onto a wet fence.

Just then, the bus stopped, and Duck got on.

Duck had to get off the bus. He was a big mess.

Duck jumped in the pond to
wash!

Duck ran and ran to get back
on the bus.

One morning, Duck sat on the bench and looked for the bus.

Duck sat and
sat, but he
did not see
the bus.

So Duck got up
to play!

Duck played on
a big hill and
fell into the
sand.

Duck played in the green grass and fell into the mud.

Duck played in the

plants and

fell onto a wet

fence.

Just then, the bus
stopped,
and Duck got on.

But duck had to get off the bus. He was a big mess.

Duck jumped in the pond to wash!

Duck ran and _ran_

to get _back_ on

the _bus_.

One morning, Duck sat on the
bench and looked for the bus.

Duck sat and sat, but he did
not see the bus.

So Duck got up to play!

Duck played on a big hill and fell into the sand.

Duck played in the green grass
and fell into the mud.

Duck played in the plants and fell onto a wet fence.

Just then, the bus stopped, and
Duck got on.

Duck had to get off the bus. He
was a big mess.

Duck jumped in the pond to wash!

Draw it

Duck ran and ran to get back
on the bus.

Activities

Read it:

Be a reading star! Ask your child or student to practice reading any Now I'm Reading!™ book out loud! Then:

- video record your child or student reading the book—and then he or she can be a television star!
- tape record your child or student reading the book—and then he or she can be on the "radio"!
- find an audience—set up chairs for family members or friends. Then, have your child or student put on a reading show by reading a book out loud to an audience!

Write it:

Practice writing by using different types of writing surfaces and utensils! Have your child or student try writing on a wipe-off board with a marker or on a chalkboard with chalk. Or, he or she can write with fun tools such as oil pastels or finger paint. Then, while he or she is using the new writing tool or surface, tell him or her a word to write. Tell your child or student just to write the word's beginning consonant if he or she can't write the whole word!

Draw it:

Make a silly partner picture! This is a two person activity. The first person draws something on a blank piece of paper. (Your child or student can even draw Duck using the instructions on the facing page.) Then, the second person adds to the picture by drawing *another* thing on the paper. Continue alternating turns drawing until you both agree that the masterpiece is complete!

A NOTE TO THE PARENTS:
When children create their own spellings for words they don't know, they are using **inventive spelling**. For the beginner, the act of writing is more important than the correctness of form. Sounding out words and predicting how they will be spelled reinforces an understanding of the connection between letters and sounds. Eventually, through experimenting with spelling patterns and repeated exposure to standard spelling, children will learn and use the correct form in their own writing. Until then, inventive spelling encourages early experimentation and self-expression in writing and nurtures a child's confidence as a writer.